Clint Faraday
58
The Murder Option

"We have a few options with these problems," Carl Wright said to the community meeting. "We can try to make them pass a law, we can make it a community project to embarrass people who do things to degrade the life here. We can do both, is what I suggest. People who throw garbage from cars or anything else on the streets have to be made responsible for breaking their bad habits.

"If anyone else has a suggestion, I'm listening!"

"You could strangle them!" Sam West said sourly. "I think I'd get a kick out of murdering that kind of trash! They make a fine community like this into something decent people want to avoid!"

You can take such things far too literally.

Contents

About the author

CD Moulton has traveled extensively over much of the world both in the music business, where he was a rock guitarist, songwriter and arranger and in an import/export business. He has been everything from a bar owner to auto salvage (junkyard) manager, longshoreman to high steel worker, orchid grower to landscaper, tropical fish farmer to commercial fisherman. He started writing books in 1983 and has published more than 350 books as of January 1, 2023. His most popular books to date are about research with orchids, though much of his science fiction and fantasy work has proven popular. He wrote the CD Grimes, PI series, and the Det. Nick Storie series, Clint Faraday series, and many other works.

He now resides in Gualaca, Chiriqui, Panamá, where he writes books, plays music with friends, does research with orchids and medicinal plants. He has lately become involved in fighting for the rights of the indigenous people, who are among his closest friends, and in fighting the extreme corruption in the courts and police in Panamá.

He offers the free e-book, *Fading Paradise*, that explains what he has been through because of the corruption.

CD is the discoverer of the Chadam Protocol for curing cancer.

Facebook page Ambrosia peruviana for cancer.

"Well, we should be able to do *something* about that!" Donna Stanton remarked stiffly. "That loud music may be alright in cities and towns where there aren't any gringos or something. *We* came here for a little peace and quiet. Those places make the nights until closing a big hellish noise!

"The real problem as I see it is that people will refuse to take *responsibility* for what they do! *No one* holds them to account! We have the noise law, but they *refuse* to enforce it!"

"The law is written where three or more people must object, then they have to enforce it. It's strong on the point that after once they'll close the place. Get three neighbors together and make the complaint where and when you can show the corruption board the law was followed on the complaint part," Carl Wright answered. "It's back to the corruption. They give the local cops ten bucks and say not to do anything. You have to go over their heads."

"We can do that!"

"What about the noise and trash and everything else certain people put us all through?" Misty Downs asked. "I mean, dogs barking and turning over trash cans. Cats howling and fighting. Everyone says that they're just animals being animals, but I insist the owner of a pet has responsibility! We have to make them accept that or get rid of the animals.

"I really don't blame the animal. After all, they *are* just animals. I blame the owner who won't take the responsibility to train or pen them up.

"Roosters crowing at godawful hours took a long time to get used to, but you can't train a rooster and they're just wild now anyhow. We did have a couple of round-ups where we paid the kids a dollar each for roosters and had chicken soup for a long time! When they get too many and too bad we can always do that again.

"Can't we have a fine or something when someone has a dog that barks and howls half the night? Can't we make cat owners, any owners, for that matter, pay for cleaning up what they destroy?

"Keep them inside at night, there's never a problem. Too obvious and simple for you?

"Those parrots a few people at this meeting have can be as bad. All you have to do is cover them and they shut up! Please!"

"I have to agree with Misty!" Gloria Felon said. "They have those dogs they *refuse* to control barking at all hours over nothing!"

"We'll have to try to work something out. We can't ask for a new law for everything. There are hundreds of wild parrots that make a lot of noise at sunrise and sunset," Carl replied. "We should just concentrate on one thing at the time. This meeting is more about trash on the streets."

"The wild parrots are in the trees mostly outside of town," Gloria sniffed. "I'm talking about the ones ten feet from you on someone's porch!"

"I agree with Carl. We can schedule a meeting about other things, but this is about trash on the streets," Harry Dickerson suggested.

"Second!" Dan Yancy cried. "We'll be here all night and won't accomplish anything at all! It always turns into that! I'd propose a law that says a meeting concentrates on what it says on the board! I, for one, can't spend two nights a week arguing about anything but what the meeting was called for!"

"For tonight anyway," Carl answered. "We can argue about other things at another time.

"We have a few options with these problems. We can try to make them pass a law, we can make it a community project to embarrass people who do things to degrade the life here. We can do both is what I suggest. Those people who throw garbage from cars or anything else on the streets have to be made responsible for breaking their bad habits.

"If anyone else has a suggestion, I'm listening!"

"You could strangle them!" Sam West said sourly. "I think I'd get a kick out of murdering that kind of trash! They make a fine community like this into something decent people want to avoid!"

The crowd laughed and it turned a bit lighter.

The meeting broke up when they said they would make it part of the Boquete Charter as an amendment that anyone caught throwing trash on the streets would be subject to doubling fines, starting with fifty dollars for a first of-fense. Non-residents would be warned the first time, then it would apply. Signs would be posted in English and Spanish saying the order began on the first of June, giving them May and a few days in April to get the word out.

The meeting broke up and everyone had coffee and cookies and talked about things that were happening with the new government now that Martinelli was president. He was just elected, and had seemed to be doing good things, but there were some very serious questions about other things. There was no doubt he had broken his promises to the Indios. That left a sour taste in the mouths of people who had backed him.

They couldn't vote, but they could make their opinions known – though that could be a long way from smart. People with sense stayed out of politics.

The meeting, as all were, was video-recorded. That would become important six years later.

"Hello, Clint," Roger Serrano, police captain in Boquete, Panamá, greeted. "I heard you were in David and took a chance that you'd help me with something."

"Yo, Rog! How are things in Snobsville?"

"Only a few are like that, but everyone has to live with it. Most are pretty good people.

"I have a very confusing type murder here. It's an old lady, Sally Bracey, who never bothered anyone. She was liked by the natives and most of the people here. I don't think she was *dis*liked by anyone, but she was poisoned. It had to be deliberate. The poison grows on the Caribbean side, mostly in The Darien and down to just north of the canal. It was in her cinnamon tea, which she drank several cups of a day.

"I have no motive, no suspects."

"Maybe it was some crazy type thing that won't be repeated."

"I think it wasn't the first. I always check the computer for these kinds of things. If there was no evidence of anything like it before, I'd just do what I could and watch for anything else.

"Clint, there were four others over the past six years. The poison was different, but everything else fit. It was people who weren't particularly disliked for any important thing. Bill Marting burned garbage and stunk up the place. There was a complaint that he let his dogs run around the neighborhood and get into people's garbage. That was two oh oh nine.

"Another I found was two oh oh nine. Amanda Stuart. She had a goat or something they made her get rid of. Nothing else.

"Ellie Pinzer, in two oh eleven, had nothing at all against her that I can find. Arthur Conan played a radio a bit too loud and he had a little Pekinese that yapped. There were no formal complaints, but it was noted at a community meeting. I think they resolved it there.

"Now, Sally Bracey. No complaints of any kind. I can't figure it. What triggers this killer?"

"It's a woman. Poison. Not absolute, but a good bet," Clint replied. "I do have a question or two. This might be one that gets away, but we can give it the old college try. If the killer stops, we probably can't get anything on her. If it's some kind of sick game where she thinks she can outsmart the police she'll be caught, but may kill others before she is so we have to try to stop it.

"I'll get up there in about three hours. My business here is almost done."

"Thanks, Clint."

Clint went to the bank to transfer two million dollars from his personal account to the CJM fund. It was money he made mostly by weird circumstance or accident. He, Judi Lum, his neighbor in Bocas, and Manny Matthews, actually Marko Bocinni, retired mob boss from California, had set up to build schools and clinics in the comarcas. He had never wanted more money than what it cost to live like he wanted to live, which was with his wife and offspring on the comarca and become one of the people there.

Several people had joked about it in the past. He was a multi-millionaire who lived in a small house on the comarca, one place in Cusapín and one near Quebrada Tula. He worked just like the other indigenos. He was actually a part of the community, not, like outside the comarca, some- one who lived in a community.

After the bank he delivered a few things to friends and relatives of friends around David, then headed for Boquete.

Boquete is a beautiful area on the side of Volcan Barú. It is at an altitude where the days are pleasantly cool in relation to David, where it is much hotter. Nights can be very cool.

Gringos have settled Boquete and are moving toward Portrerillos, a bit lower. The majority are very normal people, but a few are the snobbish type that Clint would like to smack in the chops at times.

"Why don't the people here learn proper English? After all (condescendingly), we spend our *money* here!"

Clint had recently come back at one of those. "You are living in Panamá. You came here because it's the most pleasant place you've ever found. It's beautiful and the people are warm and friendly if you'll let them be.

"The language in Panamá is Spanish. I live here so I learned the language. I live on the comarca most of the time where the language is Ngobe. I learned Ngobe.

"You are, without doubt, one of those who cry about the Latinos in the states. 'They come here where we speak English and don't even bother to learn the language!'

"Most of them do, like most gringos who come here learn Spanish.

"If it bothers you so that they don't bow and scrape because you have money, why don't you go the hell back where you came from!?"

Her husband was getting huffy when the wife's brother said, "I've heard exactly that from both of them a thousand times."

"And you'll hear it a thousand more! It's our money they live on!" the husband said.

"They lived very well, in some ways much better, for hundreds of years before you brought your arrogance and egotism here! Go back to wherever you can find people who are like you and leave us alone!"

"You trailer trash who never had anything always try to sound so outraged when anyone who has something says anything!" she snapped hotly. "You're just jealous because we've made something of our lives and you wallow in dirty ditches with the pigs!"

Tyna, who was close at the time, came to innocently say, "Clint, forgive me for interrupting you, but Judi has to get to Changuinola for the fund. She asks if you'll lend them fifteen million so they can start the new hospital construction. She says she knows it was supposed to be sent next month, but they can save almost a million if they buy the materials on a solid contract now.

"I mean, it's only fifteen million. I said you wouldn't hesitate."

"She knows she can get a lousy fifteen million anytime they need it!," Clint answered. "Why won't she believe me and talk to Juan or somebody? He can release anything up to fifty million without me having to go all over bloody hell and back! The money's just sitting there! Christ!"

It was true and was for next week except she had multiplied everything by ten. The Bigshits, as Clint et al called them, were both about to faint. The brother looked interested with a small grin on his face. Clint waved and walked away with Tyna.

The brother had been talking to a local lawyer Clint knew. He asked if Clint really had fifteen million to give to some hospital.

"He won't miss any meals if he gives away fifteen million – and he gives away a lot of money. I just can never understand that kind of person!" Gordo answered. The brother laughed and said, "I wouldn't mind wallowing in that ditch myself!"

Clint thought of that and some of the people in the area and sighed. Nothing would change. They had their club meetings about how to get the government here to give them garbage pickup and street plantings and all the things they had in the states – at no cost (and they don't pay taxes the first ten years and want the jubilado discount on everything).

Those meetings might be important if anyone could remember things from six years ago! Whoever was committing these murders would have made some kind of objections about the people she killed, surely!

Maybe she would be the kind to stay silent and "take care of things herself." He would have to look at both sides of that coin.

Corny! Maybe the club minutes would tell him something if they even kept them. Most would be careful about that so he might get a break.

He went to ask Roger about that possibility. Roger said Carl Wright was the head of the community council for the past eight or ten years and was a good person. He wasn't the "Asshole Gringo" type. The meetings were recorded. If he could spend the time he could see and hear the whole mess.

Roger took him to Carl's house. Carl said he kept all that on disk and Clint could look them over. They held the meetings monthly. There were a lot of them. Six years ago would be twelve disks. Clint had to promise to return them when he was finished. He could copy any parts he needed to his own memory stick.

He had some knowledge of computer storage and had put a hyperlink to all the times when it was more than reading the minutes and blather. The meat of the meetings would be easy to find and was about a quarter of each disk.

Clint took those and said he would need others later, but he had to find a starting place other than two oh oh nine.

Now came the boring part of detective work. The "legwork" phase where he spent hours looking at picture or reading papers or whatever.

The hyperlinks made it a lot easier. He went to the first, which was about the laws on property ownership. The second was about paving the streets and filling potholes. The third was about the recent flooding and what to do about it. The fourth was about garbage and noise. The fifth was about poor drainage. The sixth was about gardening. The seventh was about general reports on progress. The eighth was almost nothing. A complaint about a fence that was rundown and a barking dog. The ninth was about a bar and trouble there. The tenth was about the lack of protection against minors. The eleventh was about the Christmas party. The twelfth was blather.

Four, eight and nine.

He studied four. Donna Stanton, Misty Downs, Gloria Felon. Harry Dickerson might be a sleeper, or Dan Yancy. If it wasn't someone who simply sat back and listened at the meetings it would be one of those.

Not much, but a place to start. Maybe.

He would check on those people. He would have to make up some excuse to be talking to them at all. Roger was keeping quiet about his suspicions.

He called Carl to ask what the latest meeting was about. Juvenile crime – and the fact you couldn't prosecute a minor without the consent of the parents.

Talk about stupid!

It gave him a reason to be talking to people. A person who worked with the police asking about ways to get around the law.

He knew one. He would happen to drop it in each conversation and they could work it out the next meeting.

Roger gave him the addresses of his subjects. Dan Yancy moved back to Arizona three years ago, but the rest were still around.

If the killer was one of the remaining four, this might not be so hard!

Yeah! Right!

Clint looked at the neat flower garden in front of Donna Stanton's place. She was working at the side of the house with some plants. He went over to introduce himself.

"Clint Faraday? The detective who caught those international spies last month? I'm most impressed! What are you doing here? International intrigue, I hope!"

"I'm interested in the way the law here seems to protect juvenile thugs. You probably also know how I feel about that, being a Ngobe. It protects them against responsibility. That is never good! A person should have responsibility for his actions from a very young age."

"Well, I also know how you feel about the Indios and I know the Ngobe are different from the Guayme, but they steal. You know that."

"Well, yes and no. They have no ownership and will take things you aren't using. If you need them, say so. They'll bring them back. No offense.

"On the other hand, people who don't know them will claim they're all thieves and worse and won't listen to anything else because they lost something when an Indio took it. They lump all Indios into the same pen.

"If you're going to be hung as a horse thief no matter what you might as well steal a horse."

"Touché!"

"Petty theft or whatever isn't really the concern here. I'm talking about other things. The more extreme violence and such. I agree that not making a person responsible for those kinds of things is counterproductive. It makes them think they'll be free and clear no matter what. They turn eighteen and end up in the pen.

"The fact is, if you're raised without having responsibility until you're a certain age, it instills an idea that it's alright somehow. The gringo and Latin cultures breed criminals with that stupidity.

"Look at Costa Rica! If you even yell at your child, you can lose the child and even end up in jail! Look at the crime rate and the economic situation there! It's beyond moronic!"

"I wish I could argue the point. I don't believe in striking a child. I also believe that being raised in a barn will make you bray like a farm animal."

"Taking that to where you don't dare even yell at them for something is a bit extreme isn't it?"

"Again, touché! What can we do? The law is that they can't be touched!"

"The law is that they can't be touched *without the parents' consent*. It's a matter of making the parent responsible, then the child immediately has to be taught responsibility."

"How do we do that?

"Oh, you can pass an area law that holds the parents financially responsible for anything the child does. It relieves about eighty percent of the problem. Genetic criminals will always be with us, but it will take away their reinforcement, in a manner of speaking.

"It's so quiet here! I can't believe it! Most places, the culture allows, even encourages, a lot of loud music! Not even any dogs barking!"

"We've got a noise ordinance. The real problem was bars. In the daytime it's just irritating. At night it was awful! From dusk until closing time volume like it was in a football stadium! Ridiculous!

"Even a lot of the natives say it's great that it's quiet at night here."

"I can see how that would help! How did you manage to get dog owners to shut the yappers up? Those and roosters are everywhere, it seems."

"Roosters make good soup. We round them up and have free chicken for anyone when they get to be a problem.

"Dogs? They and cats were once a problem. It sort of died away. I think the objections at the community meetings made it plain to the owners that we wouldn't put up with it. They would find themselves without friends if they didn't train their pets. You can't train a rooster so that was handled another way. Chicken soup!

"I remember five years or so ago that a sour old redneck had dogs that barked all the time. He would even order them to bark to annoy people! He burned trash in his back yard. Plastic. That stinks to holy heaven!

"He used some ant poison instead of sugar or something. I think it made people stop and think that it could have been deliberate because of his attitude. Maybe, as sick as it seems, that woke some people up!"

"Do you think it was deliberate?"

"I've wondered. I really don't think so, but you also can see why someone might do something like that. Particularly if you were a very close neighbor. I'm a long way away, but could hear the damned dogs if the wind was from that way. It was annoying."

"Well, I have to talk to some more people about the juveniles and crime. You've really made this place beautiful. I have a lot of orchids on my places. Dave, a botanist friend, plants them all the time. I've sort of gotten into them."

He waved and went on. A neighbor, Charlie Parsons, was in his yard, so Clint talked with him about juvenile crime for a few minutes. His solution was to get others their age to kick hell out of them. Maybe that would slow them down!

Misty Downs was a "fluffy" older woman who liked to mother people. It was the same as with Donna Stanton except it was how beautiful she had made her home and how warm and inviting it was, showing Clint that Misty was a warm and friendly person.

Harry Dickerson was a slightly pudgy short man in his late sixties with a "babyface" and shy manner. He remembered a meeting where it was suggested that stopping certain things with new laws was beginning to constrict people too much and strangulation was a good way to stop the problem – with which he agreed – but was too extreme.

"If that Marting asshole had been strangled, I'd know damned well Sam did it, but I wouldn't be telling you about it!"

"Marting asshole?"

"Guy, real hick, named Marting. Got a teaspoon of cyanide in his iced tea. Probably an accident, but I like to think one of us had enough of his backwoodsy bullshit and put a stop to it."

"Oh. Yeah. Five or six years ago.

"Why the Sam West ... like I give a shit."

"Oh, Sam suggested strangling people like that. At a community meeting. It was one of those things where many a truth is spoken in jest.

"I had dinner with Gloria the other night. She wants to work out some way to quietly handle the problem. I agree. No big fuss. Misty wants to make a big fuss."

They talked a few minutes, then Clint went on.

So. Why was Dickerson trying to slant any suspicion to anyone else? West wasn't the type to use poison. He was the type to get a gun and blow their head off, according to Roger.

Which could be an act?

Still, nothing to hang anything on.

Gloria Felon was a bit stiffer and formal, but not to a degree that was off-putting. She was a feminist, Clint suspected.

"They should have a woman to propose their laws and then this kind of thing wouldn't be a problem!"

"Like Costa Rica? Where a man is a second class citizen because of the women presidents and their laws? Where the crime rate is a hundred times what it is here? Really? Where you can lose your children if you even yell at them? Where it's not safe to take a taxi, even? Where you're a minor in a lot of things until you're twenty five?

"Believe me, we've looked at a lot of things in a lot of places. If there's anything that does *not* work it's allowing only women *or* only men to make the laws. Life's a concession, a meeting of ideas. What we need is to hold both parents responsible in my opinion. If they're responsible by law, they'll instill responsibility in their children as a matter of practicality. If Poppa is going to have to pay a month's salary to someone his undisciplined brat robbed or broke into his place or whatever else, the kid's going to learn where that will lead!"

"Mr. Faraday, I wish I could argue the point, but I had to go to Costa Rica last year and couldn't even leave the hotel in San José to go across the street to another restaurant after eight o'clock! There was a thing in the paper about the lax enforcement and exactly that point was made. I was right there and could see it was true.

"I'll never step foot in Costa Rica again. I was there fifteen years ago and loved it. Now, uh-uh! No way!"

She thought all those men with yapping dogs should get a big dose of cyanide. That was true of several people. They should not be allowed in a community where decent people of standing lived. It was intolerable!

Luckily, there were very few like that.

Clint thought about it. If only men had been poisoned he would have suspect number one A! With three of five being women he doubted it.

Not off the list, but a lot further down.

He didn't have a main suspect. Misty was obvious. Arsenic and Old Lace. He couldn't buy it.

He couldn't reject it, either.

He never thought this was going to be an easy one.

Well, seeing he had been brought up....

Sam West was a more bullish man in his early or mid seventies. He reminded Clint of retired military. Maybe a colonel. He asked.

"Not really. I didn't like the military much. Merchant Marine, then commercial fisherman out of Galveston.

"Tell you like it is. Galveston ain't a place for a fishing base, but what the hell. I made out okay. Got into buying derelicts and redoing them. Made about sixty grand per. Three a year.

"See, there's a lot of them laying around because of the new laws. Pick up three at the time at auction. Ten grand per. Cost fifteen-twenty to refurbish as a better class live-on. Lots of people got the geetus and want out of the states anymore. Good solid boat. Plenty room. Got, say, twenty five in it, sell it for eighty.

"Got to work your ass off! Can't hire out management for the refurbish bit. They'll cut corners and your rep goes down the toilet. Been out of it for eleven years and still get lots of offers to run an operation.

"Made mine. Shove it! Ain't goin' back! Never!

"Course, they'd want to know why I had so much more than got reported if I did!"

"How much did you run?"

"Not a lot, but quality. Only pot. I wouldn't never touch nothing stronger. Like a toke or two myself and know what they claim is ninety nine percent bullshit. Booze and tobacco won't never let them change that bullshit line to the truth.

"Now, don't get me wrong. I don't believe in drivin' or any of that if you're high, but I'm against drivin' with booze even more. Don't get what they call 'aggressive' with pot. Do with booze."

Clint nodded. He wasn't getting into those arguments. As West said, nothing was going to change so long as the big booze and tobacco people were in control.

A very pretty, very sexy woman in her late twenties came to drape herself over him. She said lunch would be ready in half an hour and went back inside.

"Wife," West said. "'Magine and old fart like me with the sexiest broad in town!"

"Don't have to," Clint replied. "There she is!"

West laughed and gave Clint a high-five.

Well, he was never on the list so he didn't have to be taken off.

"What? This is going to become a case of elimination until there's just one left? You haven't really eliminated anyone yet!" Roger said.

"How true! Interesting people, though.

"Rog, there was a thing that came up and it sort of connects with something else. I'll have to get the meetings for two months before each one was, shall we say, 'Eliminated' as a problem."

"Carl said anything you need he'll give you. He's one person who busts his ass to make this a better place. He doesn't want anything like this hanging over its reputation."

Clint thought and grinned. They chatted a bit more, then Clint went to Carl's and asked for the disks of the meetings. Carl said he could figure what Clint was after by those dates. He should ask about one more, maybe.

"One more?"

"Lester Waite. A real redneck from Arkansas. Threw parties for a few of the local Indios and supplied booze. Right over the river in the fancy teak and rock house. Oh eight. Had Pitt Bulls that terrorized the neighbors, but we made him get rid of those – so he got four Dobbermans that barked all the time.”

“He was poisoned?”

“No. Rock from the bridge when he went under to throw a bag of beer cans in the river.”

“Oh. He wouldn’t eat his mushrooms?”

Carl laughed. “Something like that.”

Clint nodded and took those disks. He asked Rog about Waite. Rog agreed that could be the way it went down. There was certainly no rock that size there to fall off the bridge. He had expected Waite to get killed for some time. He didn’t fit. No one liked him. There was motive aplenty. Waite tended to be a bully on top of it. He had considered himself a superstud who the women couldn’t resist.

“Like the ones who hang a round the bar talking about the woman last night who was fantastic and wouldn’t leave him alone! He was too old to handle more than one a night anymore and she wouldn’t quit!

“Then they go to the local whorehouse and pay for it when the bar closes.”

“That’s one type Boquete has more than its share of! I have to admit that there are a lot of the big talk and no action type.”

“Well, I’ll check over these disks. I have to admit the hyperlink things are a big help – and I have to wonder if someone's depending on that to keep anyone else from finding a little thing here and there."

"Carl? No way!"

"I hope not. I like him."

Clint took the disks to his hotel and ran them on his laptop. He found the first one and reran it. It left him in the same place, but he expected that.

He made a short list of what the complaints were about against the victims and who had made remarks.

Next, Amanda Stuart had mini-pigs and a mini-goat. Misty had complained, and Yancy.

Ellie Pinzer had nine cats and took in any stray. They got loud when one was in heat and the males would fight over her. They ruined a neighbor's vegetable/spice garden. Dickerson had raised hell. It was his garden. She had been warned to keep the cats on her own property.

She was at the meeting and basically said they were just animals that had been brought there and abandoned to live on the streets and people were so callous and mean about anyone trying to right a wrong!

It was resolved that she would pay for the amounts of spices and vegetables ruined. It came to eighty five dollars. She had given

Dickerson a hundred and told him he was a sick brute and should stick the money up his ass! Gloria Felon had said it was resolved and should be forgotten. Ellie said for her to butt out. It was none of her business. She would never forget anything! It was getting hot and Carl broke it up.

Next was Waite. There had been objections about him for four meetings, starting three weeks after he moved in. After hearing the things he had done Clint felt he wouldn't mind knocking that one off himself. Give whoever did it the Good Citizenship medal! All of them, as well as nine others, had made objections against him. He had attended the last meeting two nights before he met his rock. He was always threatening people.

A big man with a blond ponytail who Clint had seen on a couple of the disks, a man who sat near the back and didn't say much, stood and said the next time the asshole SOB threatened anybody in Boquete he was going to get his sorry ass kicked from one end of town to the other.

Waite started to say something and the man grabbed him by the front of his shirt and lifted him off his feet.

"Got it, asshole?"

Waite couldn't get out of there fast enough.

Clint called Roger, who said the guy was Charlie Steinmetz. He wasn't at that meeting, but heard about it. As quiet as Charlie always was he found it hard to believe, but everyone said it happened exactly the way Clint saw on the disk.

"To tell the truth, I thought maybe Charlie handled that and didn't pursue it far."

"Where will I find Charlie?"

"Probably at Amigos at seven. He usually has two beers a night there. Everybody likes him. He's no bullshit. He might be at Millie's for lunch."

Clint turned off the computer and headed for the popular café. Charlie was there taking with two Indios and a big black man Clint had known in David.

Clint knew the Indios and greeted them in dialect. They returned the greeting and asked Charlie if Clint could join them. Charlie said, "Always room for one more. Sit!"

"Hi, Clint. what's up that you're here for?" Arvin, the black, asked.

"The juvenile crime rate. You, of all people, know about that!"

Arvin laughed. He had been a pure hellion in Bocas. Clint had done what was suggested in that first meeting. He got a couple of kids the same age (16 at the time) and had them kick hell out of him. He was told it was going to happen every time he broke into another house or tried to intimidate people who were smaller than himself. He admitted that what Clint had done made a man out of him and that he would be in prison if it hadn't happened. He was doing alright as the boss of a construction crew, a job Clint had recommended him for.

"Yeah. Just get more and bigger punks to kick hell out of them a few times. Problem solved!" He laughed along with Clint.

"Why, we can't do that! We can't answer violence with violence!" Obilio, one of the Indios, whined.

"It's the only way to answer it that works," Charlie insisted. "I've heard a lot about you, Clint. I'm Charlie."

"You're supposed to be the quiet type. Why are you promoting this senseless and counter-productive violence here? It's just *horrible*! You're nothing but a bunch of *thugs*!" Arvin replied with a shocked look.

"You got us figured!" Charlie shot back.

They joked and talked for more than an hour. Charlie didn't knock someone's brains out with any rock. He might break someone in half and toss the pieces off opposite sides of the bridge. He was a basically non-violent person, but one who would take no shit from anyone.

Clint went back to the hotel and his laptop.

Arthur Conan was the type of person almost everyone was neutral about. No real friends, no real enemies. A mention was made about his radio being too loud. He had apparently turned it down, but it had slowly gotten up to loud again. Sometimes his dogs barked. He said they only barked when someone came onto his property. They were trained. Donna Stanton said she was on the other side of the street and that the dogs barked just to be barking. The female would go on for hours sometimes. Conan said she had done that once when she was in heat. He had put her inside and made her shut up. It was maybe fifteen minutes, not hours. He came home and shut her up.

A woman they called "Mabel" said she heard the dogs and it was more than that, but not hours. Back in Indiana he would get a big fine if they barked for more than five minutes or more than a couple of times. They had that protection there!

There was an aside to that disk. Carl said he had made a discrete test. Conan couldn't hear certain types of sound and was impaired to a degree. He probably honestly didn't hear the dogs and that was why the radio was so loud. He would suggest a hearing aid to solve the problem.

Sally Bracey, no objections by anyone at the meetings, but Carl had an aside that he had a note from a member to warn her about her cats. She was starting to collect strays. He didn't say who sent the note. He had talked with her and she agreed to keep the cats inside, but she wasn't going to "abandon" them again like people had done before. He had mentioned it in the meeting, but that was all.

The woman they called "Mabel" said she would never have that problem in Indiana. They would take her cats to the Humane Society and fine her if the cats were a nuisance.

He called Carl.

"Bracey's cats? I don't ... the note? It wasn't signed. She was a bit adamant about cats. I told her they weren't abandoned. Maybe their great grandmother or such was, but they were street cats that had been around for years. We catch them and take them to the shelter in Concepcion when we can, but they're pretty smart about avoiding us. They seem to sense when we're going to round them up and manage to disappear. They breed more and more, faster than we can catch them.

"She was one of those who believed cats were super-intelligent."

"With a ten day memory. Yeah," Clint said.

"Making any progress on finding our serial killer?"

"I'm meeting some interesting people. I tend to like Charlie.

"Who's Mabel?"

"Mabel?"

"She was on a couple of the disks. Indiana had all the answers."

"Oh. Mabel Buckminster. Indiana has all the answers to everything. It was paradise. If it was warm in the winter, she would stay there, but her arthritis blah, blah, blah.

"Put everything she got when her husband died into a place here and can't figure how to get back out. She can live pretty well here on her social security, seeing she owns her home. It's just that she misses people with class, but she does try to understand that most people here didn't have the advantages she had growing up. One must make concessions."

"A Boquete Gringa. The type that makes you resented anywhere."

"We all live with what a few are."

"Boy, don't I know it!"

"She did it? I hope!"

"Outside possibility. I doubt the type would do more than talk though."

"Got a suspect?"

"A bunch!"

"Picture a closed fist with the middle finger extended."

Closing In

Clint spent the rest of the day with the disks and a few others to see how the meetings were handled. Not much else. Mabel came up a bit too often. Maybe she was just trying to get attention.

He thought about it and called Roger. He got Mabel's address and phone number. He was going to call, but thought about things she said.

"Call someone at nine o'clock in the morning?! How gauche!" He could picture it.

He went to the restaurant by the park for breakfast. They had a very good two-egg omelet and exceptional coffee. He chatted with a number of people, both natives and residents. These were a good crowd until a man got off the bus and came over. He was wearing a suit. That was a part that made Clint know he was a lawyer.

Wrong! He was a "businessman" from New Hampshire, here to teach the primitives a thing or two about construction! The footer wasn't up to grade and none of the rest of that disgusting mess would pass inspection either! He wished someone in authority here spoke English so he could teach them how to build anything. The only good thing was the construction in Boquete was better than anywhere else! Hadn't these people ever heard of the building code?

"Oh? Had any problems with your volcanoes in New Hampshire?" Clint asked innocently.

"What the hell are you prattling about? There are no volcanoes in New Hampshire!"

"You're sitting in a café on the side of one here. What would happen if you got even a little tremor in New Hampshire?"

"If things are properly up to code it wouldn't do any damage!"

"Like hell! It's built to a different code. You would have acres of rubble."

Several there spoke English, but weren't about to let the ass know that. They were giving Clint grins and thumbs up.

"That's simply not true! If it's to code, there wouldn't be that much damage!"

Sometimes things happen exactly at the right time. There was a slight tremor that made some cups rattle and some silverware bounced a bit. The whole world seemed to sway a little.

"Yee! What was that?!" from New Hampshire.

"Pardon? What was what?" No one else seemed to notice. (They did, but would play along. They were used to those small tremors. It really wasn't enough to worry about in any way.)

"You mean you didn't feel that?! It was a damned *earthquake*!"

"I think it was just ... Javier, Esta un temblor?"

"Que? Es un camion ... possiblemente. No hay camion ese pesado aqui." He was having trouble not laughing.

"What? What did he say?"

"He said he thought it was just a heavy truck going by, but there are no trucks, so, maybe. A small one."

"But ... I mean ... do you get many?"

"Many? Many what? Women?"

"No! Earthquakes! You know what I mean!"

"Temblors? A few. Usually not that light. No one notices those. It's part of living on a volcano. Once in awhile we get a five or six, but not too often."

"Seismic? Five or six? My God!"

"We're built for that. There was a seven a couple of years ago that did a little damage. Cracked some roads and a few of the newer things came down, but that's because they were built to a code for a place that doesn't have earthquakes.

"Get the point?"

"I don't believe you! A seismic five or six would devastate the area!"

"Then look it up on your fancy little computer. It was on the news. Search CNN for earth tremors the past three years.

"I have an appointment. Maybe you should book a flight back to where you know what the hell's going on! Your codes and book learning are meaningless here!"

Clint stood, paid his check and waved at the others as he left. He thought how well that one and Mabel would get along. Maybe he should play matchmaker!

What the hell? He'd never met Mabel.

On the other hand, he knew the type.

He walked around town and talked to people, bringing up things in passing, a technique Judi had taught him. Move on and see if someone has a comment, which you seem totally disinterested in. She was a genius in getting information you didn't know you gave.

"Oh, I remember Marting. I was surprised he didn't get a cup of cyanide years before!"

"Yeah. Do you think it'll rain harder? I didn't bring an umbrella."

"Ellie could be a total pain with her belief that cats were sent to teach us by God himself!"

"I guess. Isn't that an unusual color on that hibiscus?"

"Sally was usually sweet, but she could be a bitch about her cats. There was a woman a couple of years ago like her. Cats were the greatest thing in the world!

"Why, I never thought of it, but *she* died from poison, too! Maybe her cats poisoned her!"

"Reminds me. I need to get some malathion."

"Amanda. You mean Amanda Stuart? She probably suicided when they made her get rid of that smelly goat!"

"Goat? Who? Her husband? You say he was a smelly goat?

"I see they finally cleaned up from when the river flooded."

"Arthur Conan? Now, I don't *know*, but I've *heard* that he was a bit fond of little girls! I mean *little* girls! Ten or twelve years old!"

"Uh-huh. Did you see that King Arthur and the Roundtable thing on TV last week?"

At ten sharp he called Mabel. He said he was in town and a friend from Indiana said there was a woman in Boquete from Indiana. A Mrs. John Buckminster. Was she the one?

"I'm Mabel Buckminster. You are?"

"Oh! Sorry! I really do know better. Clinton Faraday."

"Yes. One tends to forget the finer points of culture when they're in these ... places.

"Are you in Boquete?"

"Yes. I'm working with the government here. Trying to get some better services and so forth. Hopeless task, it sometimes seems."

"You don't sound like Indiana."

"Oh! No! I'm from Florida. I once worked with a John Buckminster on a project. I took a chance you could be related. I don't know many from the states here. I've been here some years."

"Clinton Faraday ... I seem to have heard the name before?"

"Yes. I've had some involvement with the police in some things and get my name on the news, much to my chagrin."

"Police? I can imagine! Involvement?"

"Oh! Not *that* way! I am asked at times for aid in solving a crime. I do seem to have a talent. Murders, you know."

"I'm sure such things don't interest me, other than a few books by personages such as Lady Agatha. Works of quality, if you can call a murder mystery a work of quality.

"I'm just awful, but I do like some of those better ones!" She sounded almost human with the last sentence.

"It's the puzzle, you see. I like to solve puzzles. It keeps life interesting," Clint replied.

"Heaven knows we need some kind of interest! Life here can be tedious."

"Well, I always say life is what you make it. I keep busy and have found interests. I have a famous friend who writes murder mysteries. He's also a musician and a botanist. He's in his seventies and roams the jungles with research concerning orchids."

"Dave? He has guested at the garden club. He's what we would call a real character back home. He is knowledgeable about orchids, but he isn't among the classes, if you know what I mean."

"That's what's so strange. He actually is! He's actually royalty back in England. His great grandfather was Earl Norwood.

"His interests are in other things. He's certainly made life interesting for himself! Most people would be suicidal if only a few of the things I've seen happened to them! He shrugs it off and says he's not really interested in such things.

"Well, I'm being paged! Back to the old grind, as they say! I wish you the best!"

"And I, you. It's a pity we couldn't meet for tea or something, but, c'est la vie!"

He rang off. She didn't kill anybody. She was more the victim type – if this were an Agatha Christie novel.

He could concentrate on the four he'd started with. Donna Stanton, Misty Downs, Gloria Felon and Harry Dickerson. Carl was still a far outside possibility.

He went back to the hotel to study a bit more. He wanted to eliminate anyone he reasonably could.

He had concentrated on what was said before more than on the people themselves. This time he studied the people in the videos.

On the first one Donna Stanton was clearly upset. Misty Downs seemed to become angered, then cool off almost immediately. Charlie was in the back and one shot showed him rolling his eyes when Misty was talking. Gloria had her lips pressed together tightly, apparently controlling herself from saying too much. Yancy was mostly looking frustrated. West was a little irritated, then amused. Carl seemed amused at times and a bit irritated at times.

The second, Donna didn't participate much. She looked very thoughtful at points. Charlie looked tired. Carl looked sympathetic, but angered, a few times. Misty looked mostly frustrated.

Next, Donna didn't participate. Gloria had the tight-lipped look. Harry was, as before, simply observing. Carl was mostly frustrated. Misty was concerned to aghast.

Same the rest.

Clint looked back through the dates on the disks and had an idea. He called Carl for the disks of the meetings just after the deaths. He went to pick them up, then to talk with Roger.

The meeting after Marting was subdued. He had died just three days before that meeting. It was brought up at the first then not mentioned again.

Carl made the announcement and was just reading a paper. Misty looked shocked (a bit overdone? She knew it for three days). Charlie gave a victory sign (?). Harry looked satisfied. Gloria was watching the reactions of the others. Donna looked satisfied.

Amanda Stuart. A week before the meeting. Not much reaction from anyone.

Waite. The night after his rock. All of them seemed surprised, to a degree. West said, "Thank you, God!" Donna sighed and looked satisfied. Misty was all shock. Gloria was watching the others. Carl said half the reason the meeting was called was gone.

Ellie Pinzer. Four days after her death. A little sadness from some, same for the others.

Arthur Conan. The day after his death. Carl looked unsurprised and nodded. Charlie nodded. Misty looked very satisfied. Gloria seemed happy about it. Donna looked confused, but not sad.

Sally Bracey. Just two days after her death. Everyone looked saddened. They all said a few words. Everyone seemed to have liked her.

Clint thought that one was different. He had seen or heard something. Something wasn't right!

Carl read the notice and said she would be a great loss to them all. She had been active about the community, if in an off-screen way.

Misty was crying and said Sally was always there when anyone needed a friend and she would miss her terribly.

Then the killer said the wrong thing.

Clint sat back. He ran the rest of the meeting and thought, then sighed.

He knew who was killing people, but he knew he couldn't prove a thing with what he had. A statement at a time when it could be taken in several ways wasn't much use in court even here where they didn't have fifty technicalities for the lawyers to argue.

He thought, then decided he would try a trick or two. He called Carl to ask when the next meeting was to be held. Next Thursday.

He would use the five days to bring things together. He would go to the meeting and would explain ... would try to make something happen.

He would see where each of them were in the past. The poison used on Bracey wasn't something that you could get anywhere except where it was growing naturally. The mouth of the canal and in the Comarca Cuna Yala and on to almost Colombia on the Caribbean coast.

Colón?

He called his friend in the comarca who was studying witchcraft and voodoo as practiced in the country. It was a close relative to belladonna or datura. It was used in the ceremonies and to get rid of any people who were bothering you. Voodoo used a lot of poisons.

"Along the lake and bay, but I doubt much in Colón, the city. If it's a gringo who used it, it would be San Blas or somewhere."

A lot of tourists went to San Blas.

He called Roger and asked if he had the copies of their passports or other travel records. Roger would check the computer system for the use of residency papers or passports.

The poison used before that was a form of organic poison, a type of mushroom.

Clint remembered the line used about Waite. He got a rock to the head because he wouldn't eat his mushrooms. An old joke.

Cyanide was easy to get, but could be organic. Casaba, or tapioca, was full of cyanide. It had to be reacted away. Roger had said it was ant poison, which was sodium cyanide, mostly.

Roger reported that only Gloria Felon had been to San Blas. Most of them had been in Colón at one time or another.

"Any investigation held into the cyanide that killed Marting?"

"Ant poison. He had some in his bodega. A lot of people have it. Arieles.

"Are you working from a definite lead or still looking for something?"

"I know who did it. I'm trying to find a way to prosecute her. What I have is a statement that could be taken several ways plus the way she sometimes acted at the meetings."

"Carl said Felon said something that had him wondering. Her?"

"Yeah. She knows she screwed up, I think. She's intelligent. I hope she's not going to try to kill off anyone who might connect what she said with anything else. Tell Carl to be damned careful! She's not exactly the sanest person living in Boquete."

"I really don't think she'd kill Carl or any of the others. She's after specific people of a specific type."

"Her statement was about doing something you don't want to do to people you don't want to harm, but such things can be necessary to the overall good of the community. She tried to make it sound like she was talking about Sally, but it doesn't make sense if you think about it. Sally didn't do anything to anybody.

"I think it was about the cats. She liked Sally, but she set out to get rid of people whose animals caused problems and had to kill her to not break the plan. She felt it was successful.

Getting rid of the others really did make the community a more pleasant place to live."

"Yech!"

"Well, I have to put a little more together, then go to a Boquete Community Club meeting. You are cordially invited to attend that meeting next Thursday at four o'clock."

"Wouldn't miss it!"

Clint decided to go into David to finish what business he had there, then would go back to Boquete for the meeting. He would put it all together so that it would look a lot more solid than it actually was.

Clint called Tyna and talked for more than an hour. He wanted to go home and forget about this mess. His son, Nito, was doing very well in school and his daughter was practicing medicine. She would get her degree in two years, but was studying the Indio natural methods. Mathilde, the local medicine woman, was teaching her a lot, but she didn't have the psy power or whatever it was Mathilde had.

Nito was studying several different fields, which was his nature. According to reports he was excelling at most and was above average in all of them.

Clint visited with people he knew and helped Sergio, from the police academy in Panamá

City, with a new curriculum for homicide investigation courses and techniques. Sergio had recently been promoted from a cop to the position. He wanted to settle down with his wife and children. The police are rotated, so that was a problem when he was an investigator and chief in different places every two years.

While he was in David he checked on what was happening with Dave's problem of having his land stolen. Nothing. He wrote a book about it that is distributed free to investors and would-be investors in Panamá. The reaction, instead of bringing about an investigation as it would in other places, was to stonewall even harder. The corrupt idiots didn't have the sense to know that was another chapter in *Fading Paradise*!

He went to all the places he used to go when he was operating out of Bocas and David. It was surprising how many old faces were still around. Some had died or moved, but the same crowd was at the same places. It was like he walked out yesterday and back in today. Same people, same stories. It was depressing. He was glad he hadn't retired his mind when he retired from the private detective business.

Retired? He never had the cases in Florida! He did at least triple the detective work since he retired!

He was in better condition for that. People who met him for the first time who knew about him from the news and such thought he was the famous Clint Faraday's son. Clint Faraday Sr. had to be close to eighty. Tis guy didn't look over fifty!

Dave was in his place in Gualaca, just forty minutes away, so he spent a couple of days and a night there. Dave was over eighty and still active. Time was wearing at him, though. He used to walk thirty or forty kilometers a day when he wasn't writing or doing music. He was tiring after about twenty five now.

They had a grand old reunion. Students kept dropping by. Dave spent all he had on sending deserving poor kids to university. It had grown to where he had twenty seven in school at the moment. Three were just graduated. He would find three more.

Dave spent a lot of time on the comarca. Clint warned him that he was getting older. He would drop dead somewhere out in the jungle and no one would even know about it for months!

"Perfect!" was the answer. Clint gave him the bird.

"Dave, what do you know about the datura poison around San Blas?"

"It's a stronger *Datura metel. Metel* acts like a truth serum and narcotic that gives you a hangover. That one can kill you pretty fast. It might be a pleasant way to go. It *is* a narcotic. Lots of scopolamine and atropine."

"Easy to get?"

"If you know what it looks like. It's in a lot of gardens. It's an Angel Trumpet. Pretty."

There was no way to trace who might have some of that. All you needed was a few seeds.

He discussed the case with Dave. Dave said he couldn't agree to such an extreme method, but barking dogs and howling cats made him want to knock off a few pet owners who had no respect for their neighbors. If they did, they'd train their pets. A rolled up newspaper and a whack when they barked for no reason for dogs. It didn't hurt them, but they learned.

Cats? Throw water on them. They hated it!

Dave has an answer for anything. He's only wrong a little more than half the time, according to him.

He spent a day in Puerto Armuelles. Manny had a lot of land near there and Clint had helped set up a mine with a Mexican hood who moved there and became, like Manny/Marko, a pillar of the community. He reminisced about the cases he had there with old friends. He couldn't help but realize that the term fit in more than one way anymore.

Thursday morning he headed for Boquete. It seemed that Gloria Felon had gone on a trip somewhere just yesterday. No one knew when she'd be back. It was a surprise to everyone!

Except Clint. He gave it fifty-fifty from the first that she'd run instead of wait to see if he actually had anything.

Roger said he saw her get on the bus for David, but didn't pay much attention. She was acting normally. Most people in Boquete did their heavy shopping in David, where prices were about half those in Boquete.

Clint also figured another thing about Felon. She'd be back!

But when?

He went to the meeting. Carl asked him to explain about the laws that made it possible for them to hold the parents responsible for the damages their minor children caused.

That was easy enough. All they had to do was pass a rule on the charter and give thirty days notice that they were going to enforce it to the letter. It applied to anyone within the town limits.

"A lot of them live outside," a man argued. "How will we hold them responsible for anything their brats do?"

"You have the 'undesirable' clause. I've read it. Declare them undesirable and don't allow them to come into Boquete for any reason. If their kids come into town, Roger will have to arrest them and take them to David. The parents will have to go to David to get them. It will make it smarter and easier for them to discipline their kids."

"We can try it. I' willing to try anything that might work," Carl said. "Vote?"

It carried with an almost unanimous vote.

Then Clint went back to the comarca to be with his wife. Roger would call when Gloria came back.

"Clint? She's back!" Roger announced three weeks later. "She's decided you can't touch her I think."

"She may be right, but I'll try. I'll be there tomorrow afternoon."

Clint told Tyna what was happening as it happened. She expected him to be gone again at anytime. She would pack a few things in the morning and he would be gone. She was used to it. They had tonight!

Clint parked outside the police station and went in. Roger greeted him and asked what the plan was. Clint said they'd play it mostly by ear. He wasn't at all sure he could shake her to admitting anything, but he'd give it a try.

"Where did she go? Do you know?" Clint asked.

"To David. Los Abanicos, I believe they said."

Clint nodded. He said he'd go visiting. Maybe he could do the unexpected and throw her timing off. Or something. He said he had an idea.

He drove to park across from her gate. She was standing on the porch. She said it was a nice day. No rain for a change.

Try a shocker.

"Smooth rocks take prints. Did you know that?

"I guess not."

She laughed. "Then you know I didn't do that one, huh?"

Something connected. Dickerson had dinner with her. Dickerson seemed to be trying to slant his suspicions.

"No. Dickerson. An alliance. That was the only one he did."

It hit the target! She was looking a bit trapped and confused. She recovered.

"Harry? I wondered about that. He seems so shy, but we dated a few times and I know he's a lot deeper than he at first seems."

"You shouldn't have said the things you did when Sally died. We knew Dickerson didn't do any of the other killings. He's not the poisoner psychology at all. To as much as admit that you liked Sally and didn't want to hurt her, but some things must be done like it or not was a giveaway that couldn't be ignored.

"You realize you were trying to justify yourself. I don't think you managed to convince yourself that Sally was justified."

"No, Mr. Faraday, I don't think Sally was justified. I think I am in dire need of psychiatric counseling. When I made that stupid little speech I found it was ... I knew right then I had gone too far and was insane. I'm willing to admit it. I understand that I need help."

"Yes, but it's too late. They don't much care for an insanity defense here. You can get psychiatric help while you're in prison, but you don't go to a nice comfortable hospital to lay around until some quack declares you cured. After a state psychiatrist says you're cured you might get a reduction, but you'll serve the time until then."

She studied him a moment. "So I won't escape what you people call justice. All I did was get rid of some people no one else had the guts to get rid of! It was for the community, not for me!"

"Up until Sally, I might have some sympathy for you. Not now. I never met any of them. It seems extreme to kill someone who hasn't trained a dog. You could use the noise ordinance you had passed to make it too expensive for them *not* to train their pets."

"Marting?"

"I'd probably not find convincing evidence in his case – but you didn't do that one."

"Should I collect a few things? Are you going to arrest me? I know you have the authority."

"No. Roger will come for you later. I have to talk to Dickerson. If you refuse testimony against him, we can't prove he was the only one to handle that rock. If we could, Roger would have arrested him long ago."

"I would never testify to anything. He's a very sweet man. He treats women with respect.

"I'll get everything in order and fix the house up so it won't deteriorate before I find someone to stay here until I'm released."

She turned and went inside. Clint shook his head and got in his car to go find Dickerson. He would be advised to say nothing. They couldn't prove anything as things stood. Don't hand the police material they would use against him.

Clint could understand why Dickerson would want to kill such as Marting. He was the shy student type and Marting was the bully. That kind of thing turned around on the bully far more often than was known.

This was all about psychological types. Felon was neurotic to the point of insanity. Dickerson was pushed too far as a youth and it exploded on him with Marting when Marting threatened him at that meeting. Marting was the bully type. He wouldn't threaten Charlie or West. They were his size and could take him, as Charlie had shown.

Clint hadn't expected the easy solution. Felon probably really did know she was nuts. Maybe they could help her.

Very little in this one was something he would expect. He wasn't at all satisfied with the case. He knew he had solved it and that the right ones were caught.

It just seemed such a waste!

"Clint! Roger from Boquete on the phone!"

It was only eight days since he talked with Gloria and Harry. Not a lot of time is wasted in Panamá with cases where there is a confession and evidence. Gloria got six years and psychiatric counseling. They really couldn't convict Harry of anything with the evidence they had.

"She was very cooperative with the court, which is why only six years. She has someone staying in her house as housesitter. Very nice people from Virginia. They'll stay in Panamá when she gets out.

"I predict she will be declared cured in less than two years. She'll serve two and be back.

"No one here holds anything against her for most of it. They do hold Sally against her.

"How are things in Cusapín?"

"I suppose they're going along as usual. Fine. I'm in Quebrada Tula for a couple of months.

"How're the rest of the people there? Most of them were pretty regular people, but that may just be the ones I met. I have met a couple from there who are royal pains in the ass."

"They're doing alright. You suggested that charter restriction about responsibility for the brats, which is causing some problems for me. I had to take those Chevara brothers to David. The father was mad as a hornet. He was told he would pay for the damage when the brothers broke into the Morrison house and for the forty two inch TV they ruined when they stole it. The whole family was declared undesirable. I had to take Papa into David where they fined him fifty dollars for coming into town after warning. It's sinking in that we're serious about that.

"Well, have to go! Charlie is throwing a party for everyone. He's able to get the gringos and the Indios together where they have a good time and no one gets sloppy drunk. The gringos go away with a better understanding. They get along much better.

"Things get better when you come to town. You're welcome anytime!"

"Maybe next year. Or the next."

C. D. Moulton's works are available on most major outlets as printed or e-books. CD writes the CD Grimes, PI, mysteries, the Det. Lt. Nick Storie mysteries, the Clint Faraday mysteries, the Flight of the Maita science fiction series, books on orchid culture and many others of many types. Mystery, adventure, intrigue, science fiction, humor, fantasy, paranormal, mild erotica, and factual.